Mini

The Daily Telegraph

Competition 2001

devised and edited by

BRIAN ALDISS

foreword by
JOANNA LUMLEY

drawings by
QUENTIN BLAKE

in support of the
ARVON FOUNDATION

supported by the

JERWOOD
FOUNDATION
CHARITABLE FOUNDATION

ENITHARMON PRESS

First published in 2001 by
Enitharmon Press
36 St George's Avenue, London N7 0HD

Distributed in Europe by Littlehampton Book Services
through Signature Book Representation
2 Little Peter Street, Manchester M15 4PS

British Library Cataloguing-in-Publication Data. A catalogue record for this
book is available from the British Library.

ISBN 1 900564 77 7

Typeset by Colin Etheridge
Printed in Great Britain by The Cromwell Press, Trowbridge, Wiltshire

Contents

Foreword

I suppose part, or all, of the attraction lies in the rigidity of the rules: exactly fifty words to tell a story. You can see the size of the desired creation in your mind's eye, in a formula as inexorable as that of a haiku. Such a tiny quota! More than the haiku's seventeen syllables, of course, but even so pretty stingy.

Taking up a pen you move closer (you are dragged by the neck) and slam! You're hooked and ideas start scrambling towards the nozzle of the brain, words waiting to be squeezed out in the exact number, counted, traded, discarded, hunted down, dithered over while your story stands by, impatiently waiting for its tailor-made apparel to be selected. The story, or the idea, the kernel, must come first – it must be so sweet and sharp and delicious – in fact, it has to become a bonne bouche, a chocolate truffle, so attractive and irresistible and tiny, but at the same time completely satisfying.

The construction might be in easy narrative, recklessly uncompressed (how will it all fit in?): a staccato sketch, mere shorthand notes with a punchline as unexpected as Mike Tyson's right; cunningly composed wordplay with internal rhymes and resonances; sheer poetry; but always a story, with a beginning, a middle and an end. It might be a love story, a whodunnit, a biography, even a history of the universe, for heaven's sake, but always the strangely accommodating fifty words. Lovely English language!

I don't suppose it would work as well in any other tongue, except Latin.

From the way I write you must be able to tell I'm an addict. I entered the very first mini-saga competition and found that winning a prize (I didn't) wasn't the goal – but pleasing or charming the judges was. There is intense pleasure and satisfaction in a world in miniature: the attraction of looking into dolls' houses, lying down to observe train sets, toy soldiers, the miniature portraits of Nicholas Hilliard, the distorted interior of snowdomes, where snowflakes the size of taxicabs fall softly on New York City, landmarks squashed together in a glassy summation of life. It is the universe and all mankind seen through the wrong end of a telescope; or a section of a familiar painting hugely magnified. I think Gerard Manley Hopkins would have celebrated this form of composition: God be praised for mini-saga rules – (but slide a comma in after 'praised' and you can extract a different spin). The secret weapon lies in the majestic competence of the words themselves, and in all the armoury of grammar and punctuation.

I think the mini-saga appeals to a certain kind of mind, but just as a hypothetical contestant begins to emerge you are floored by an entry written by a child. And then you think: is it worth writing anything *longer*? Aren't *very* slim novels immensely appealing? My father always used to say 'Ah! A lovely short book!' as he sat amongst piles of tomes too heavy to hold in one hand. No, of course we want books and chapters and sequels – it's just the beauty of these tiny masterpieces that dazzles the mind.

Give each one, when you read it, its full time: some are so clever you find you've overlooked a jewel if you read at speed. I should warn you – you may find you are haunted by a particular story: there is one in this collection that won't leave my mind. No matter which one: it's not necessarily the 'best', but it's gone into my brain the way only a mini-saga can. Bon appetit.

JOANNA LUMLEY

Introduction

This is the sixth Mini-saga competition run by the *Daily Telegraph* and the fifth anthology compiled from the best entries. How surprising that the word has not yet found its way into an Oxford dictionary!

The idea for a fifty-word, all-holds-barred story came to me early in the nineteen-eighties. I was then engaged in writing a trilogy of three rather long novels. The vision of something short – to be written in a minute, or five – was naturally inviting. I rang the *Telegraph*; they took it up and ran with it. In fact, they ran with the first competition in 1982. We had thirty-two thousand entries.

It must have brought the newspaper almost to a halt. But no, it survived and ran the competition again in 1985. This time, we collaborated with BBC Radio 4's *Today* programme. We netted almost fifty thousand entries. What does one deduce from this? It is encouraging that people still write, or have a firm belief that they can write. One of our judges on that second occasion was Brian Redhead, a stalwart of *Today* – just as we had his successor, the charming and perceptive John Humphrys, as a judge last time.

We felt a lot of talent was running to waste. Arrangements were made to publish an anthology of the best mini-sagas. I edited it and have edited every anthology since. This is our fifth anthology.

It was in 1997, with the fourth competition, that we threw in our lot with the Arvon Foundation. There is now an entry fee, which goes to the Foundation. The Foundation teaches would-be writers to write and writers to be better writers. I sometimes feel I am forging a rod for my own back . . .

For this sixth competition, we assembled some excellent judges: Quentin Blake, whose wonderful drawings enliven this book, Christopher Howse, Joanna Lumley, Blake Morrison and me; with Saul Hyman of Arvon to keep us all under control. The final judging took all morning. We were firm and vacillating by turns, before we arrived at what we all felt were fair, just and inspired decisions.

I begin to worry that posterity may remember me only as the inventor of the mini-saga, despite all my novels, short stories, poetry, and non-fiction. Here's a mini-saga about this neurosis:

The Fruits of Research

A solemn committee in the Twenty-Second Century.

'Our History of English Literature will be definitive, now that there are no more books,' gurgled a junior editor.

'Yet we're stuck already in the "A"s,' grumbled another.

'Who on Earth was – er, *Aldiss*?'

'Why, the Inventor of the Mini-saga,' snapped a know-all.

This story illustrates one of our benevolent get-outs, a good deed shining in a naughty set of restrictions. Hyphenated words can count as either one word or two.

Many reservations crop up when one is judging. While the use of clipped grammar is understandable, considering the narrow space permitted, it is clearly better to write natural English. You know the kind of unnatural thing: 'His marriage. Pretty young wife, parson's daughter. Their children. His affair. The divorce. Sorrow. Wife miserable. Chap comes in car. A kiss. Happiness! He meanwhile, wretched, broke. Drink. Drugs. She out with new husband, stinking rich, steps over old husband lying in gutter. Says, "Awful drop-outs! Should be locked up."'

Such stuttering tales often have very long titles, such as, 'Some Marriages End Happily for Some People After the Break-Up and For Some Not'. (Not quite fifteen words . . .)

Subjects have not changed greatly since our first anthology. There are still no stories about the euro. Not a lot of humour. One well-stocked category which has vanished, happily, is the Post-Catastrophe story; but you will find an effective survivor or two in these pages. Domestic stories are very frequent. I like stories in which the imagination is stretched farther – to the distant past or the distant future.

Literate writing and short titles tend to fare best. As for subject matter, it is as well to remember that most stories will concern a man and a woman, or a husband and wife, or partners. It is not the most original of themes. Judges are unenthused when one partner murders the other; a lot of blood can be contained in fifty words. Judges are unenthused about those entries in which it is revealed that a dog has been telling the story, or the cat. And of course judges are unenthused when a story contains forty-nine words, or fifty-one.

That's the devil of mini-sagas: Not only do you have to be able to write, you have to be able to count accurately!

One category of story always turns up, and is not too likely to win a prize: the Adam and Eve story. It has been done to death. Here's a mini-saga about it:

The Leniency of the Lord Almighty

'Next, we came to my least favourite kind of mini-saga,' said God, to the trillions listening.

'I refer to the mini-sagas about Adam and Eve: clichés, nothing more.'

Catching sight of the pair, lurking on a distant cloud, 'Course, it's nice to know you're still popular down below,' he grinned.

Many thanks go to all the brave entrants of the competition, to our charming judges, to the *Telegraph*, and also the Arvon Foundation organisers, whose assistance made a challenging if enjoyable task simply enjoyable.

And particular thanks and congratulations to the winners. To other contributors also included here – well done, better luck next time!

BRIAN ALDISS

Special

Jessica

Once a long, long time ago a young man called
William set out to find a wife. The only problem
was he could say only one word – 'Jessica'.
Ten days later he met a beautiful and loving girl
named Jessica. When he saw her he could say
everything about love.

JAMIE TERRILL (aged 9)
Llanfyllin

Special Category

Human Nature

Silence is Golden

'You talk too much,' he said.

She learnt silence.

In secret she wrote a novel.

The words tumbled like young monkeys across the pages.

She was published, won a prestigious prize. She became famous.

'Why did you not tell me?' he demanded to know.

She said nothing, but she smiled.

ULLA CORKILL
Peel, Isle of Man

You Only Get What You Pay For

If a picture paints a thousand words . . . what could I do with fifty?

I mixed my paints. I cut the canvas down to size.

I know you were dissatisfied with the portrait.

You refused to pay me. But your left ear is really *the* left ear of all left ears.

MARK HILL
Rodmell

Commended

Penny for Your Thoughts

'Spare change sir?' asked the gaunt adolescent.

Sir, flummoxed, fumbled and found a quid.

'There's snow tonight, not sleeping out
I hope?'

'Nah, down the airport, it's warm and hassle
free.'

Sir paused. 'Look, I've got a spare bed.'

'What? You a Christian or a pervert?'

'Neither, I'm a father.'

DAVID LAMMY M.P.

Commissioned Story

A Life

Joey, third of five, left home at sixteen, travelled
the country and wound up in Nottingham with a
wife and kids. They do shifts, the kids play out
and ends never meet. Sometimes he'd give
anything to walk away but he knows she's only got
a year and she doesn't.

JANE ROSENBERG
Brighton

Commended

By a Thread

Theseus decided. Sailed to Crete and ingratiated himself with a traitor.

Without fear along the tortuous route, thanks to the secret weapon, he arrived and slew the powerful brute.

Really grateful for her help, he left the island with informant, Ariadne. He nevertheless abandoned her, on Naxos, en route home.

Sylvia Colato
Staines

Just One Big Happy Family . . .

Big family, very close;
   'I've made a will.'
   'We don't want your money, Mum.'
   They didn't, till she died and 'The Cats'
League' got it!
   Except for the ornaments.
   'And what's *she* doing with that?'
   'I bought that!'
   Still a big family . . . but not close anymore.
   Don't even talk now!

EDDIE GASKILL
Rainham

When It's Time to Go – Go With a Bang

George walked away from his office and colleagues for the last time.

After forty years of work he was given a five minute presentation and a retirement gift. What use did he have for another clock?

Later a bomb destroyed his old office entirely. His gift proved useful after all.

PAUL BOWERS
Chandlers Ford

Scrabble

For years the same Sunday evening ritual.
His aim: to win. She always let him. Best not
to argue.

Arthritic fingers laid out his final word:
'CAPTIVE'. (Fifty bonus points!)

But victory could still be hers: she arranged
her letters to form 'AFFAIR'. With a sigh, she
settled on 'IF'.

EMMA SOUNDY
London N6

Highly Commended

No Contest!

'You only live once!' he thought. But, what would he lose?

His cosy cottage, ramshackle shed, faithful Reliant, his totally irreplaceable friends . . .

The answer was 'No'. In the shed, lighting his pipe with the £20,000,000 lottery ticket, he savoured the smoke curling lazily upwards in a beam of sunlight.

Peace!

EDWARD LANE
Otham

Material Gains

His tailoring business was coming apart at the seams. How to pay his debts?

He looked around his shop. Inspiration!

He placed adverts in national papers:

'Cut your household bills in half! Send £20.'

They sent him money. He sent back – scissors.

He'd stitched them up.

They sent him down.

MATTHEW DUNN
London SW7

Commended

Ambition

She marked him: married and manipulated him.
Subtly undermining his family and substituting
her own. Eventually she persuaded everyone that
he was losing his grip on reality so she could
complete her reverse take-over. He was sad.
She was vilified.

   Had she been in industry she would have been
knighted.

JULIA DE NAHLIK
Gillingham

The Boxer They Feared

He strolled with ease, followed by those who trained him well.

Perfect. Unbeaten. Unbeatable?

His rival was young, edgy and in danger. Of death they claimed.

A bell was heard and they began. Thirty seconds later it was over.

The unbeatable is beaten.

I can't remember his name. Nobody can.

PAUL GIMÉNEZ
Marchwood

One Man's Justice Prevails

He was always surly and taciturn. He never spoke to the other prisoners, and only to the warders when necessary.

He knew who the real murderer was, and on release found him and killed him.

This time he was a cheerful, model inmate, liked by both warders and fellow prisoners.

M. WYNN-TAYLOR
Hillingdon

Trappings
(Worth Her Weight)

'Lost property.'

He handed over a wallet. 'There's several hundred quid, platinum Amex, licence . . .'

The attendant smiled ruefully.

'Where did you find it?'

'It's mine. What if I can't measure up to all this?'

The woman blinked her confusion.

'But it's not lost.'

'It is now,' he said, walking away.

ROSEMARY HARRIS
London NW5

Flames at the Persian Gates, 331 BC

Fifteen thousand marched on Persepolis
for Alexander, grim-faced
dreamed of Xerxes' throne
Doom came upon the ancient kings
soaked earth bloody
great gates cast down
Now Alexander in your rock sarcophagus
no dust breath stirs your bones
tourists depart
goats sniff past
none to look on your deeds and despair.

NATASHA OSTOVAR
London N4

Commended

Parsing Fancy

Two grammarians (she: progressive; he:
conditionally perfect) concatenated at a
partycule. Envisioning verbing him transitively
in every conjugation, she prepositioned him.

His regular declensions were irreflexive,
'No mere object comparatively passive to
inverted commerce'.

Eyes dotted, she split his infinitive.
Inevitably, he intransitively verbed to a
She should have noun.

M. J. EVANS
Southwick

Fit for Purpose

She was a topless model, luscious and lissome,
popular with the Press, who liked to keep abreast
of events.

She married, gave birth to a son, and retired.

Enjoying being a mother, she discreetly breast-
fed her child in a restaurant and was asked to
leave. She was embarrassing the clientele.

MURIEL BERRY
Cadishead Moss

Futuristic

A Never-to-be-forgotten Name in Space Exploration

Joe Warburton, astronaut, craved the fame accorded to Gagarin and Armstrong.

As he bounced across the lunar surface, marvelling at the experience, he crunched the capsule secreted under his tongue.

Within minutes, his name would be flashed around the world – 'Joe Warburton, the first man to die on the moon.'

JANET SLADDEN
West Wickham

Commended

The Last Discovery

An asteroid of phenomenal dimensions was heading towards Earth. It had been shifted from its old trajectory by the sun.

One person saw it in his solar observatory against the glare of the sun. He could see it was an asteroid.

By then, it was too late to tell anybody.

ANTONY WISSON (aged 16)
East Cowes

Universal Sufferage

'It's so boring,' we said. 'We can't be bothered. Anyway, they're all the same. What difference will it make?'

So we stayed at home and watched TV or went to the pub and drank our beer and Chardonnay.

One day, the Militia took over. And now we're dying to vote.

HELEN YEOWART
Woodford

Colony 4

As the star ship hit warp speed Jake studied the
in-flight brochure. He didn't want to move
home, away from everything he'd ever known –
live on Colony 4 – some reclaimed rock.

'It'll be OK,' Mum reassured him.

'Yeh,' he said despondently as they docked on
planet Earth.

GILL HOLLAND
Corfe Mullen

Incest?

I realised at the funeral that I couldn't live without Isabelle, but having her cloned only made it worse.

How could I have anticipated the madness of changing my dead wife's nappies, or the heartbreak of watching my 'daughter' grow up and go out with other men, instead of me?

KATRINA STIFF
Brighton

Cyberlove

They met in cyberspace. For months they chatted in chatrooms and sent e-mails. They attached .doc files and .jpg pictures. They fell in love and promised eternal connection.

Then they exchanged a virus. Their discs crashed and could not be recovered. Now their love exists only in inaccessible corrupted memory.

PATRICK O'CONNOR
Stevenage

A Class-Project on The Beatles

'Let's do a project on The Beatles, class?' Blank faces. A small voice said:

'They are very old. Granddad remembers their music. He wore their shoes.'

'Shoes?'

'Yeh, pointy shoes. One Beatle was murdered.'

'Murdered!'

'In America. John something.'

'My Dad will know.'

'He's too young.'

The teacher turned pale.

TERRY McDONAGH
Hamburg, Germany

Commended

Business As Usual

The war had ended years ago.

I drove down the pot-holed motorway carefully. The spare tyre in the boot was the last one. I arrived at the client's site and cobbled together a fix for his computer.

The chickens I got in payment would keep me for a week.

PETER BANKS
Oldbury

Second Prize

Pest Control

It took him nearly a week to make.

But it became infested. Rotten and riddled.

Reluctantly, the old chap reached for the 'phone.

The exterminators came; did their stuff.

'Wise to call us, sir,' their chief assured him.

'Nice planet like this – you just can't risk human beings on it.'

JOHN MACHIN
Congleton

The Beginning of the End

My son, Adam, first mentioned his nightly visitors weeks ago. I barely listened, smiling at his fertile imagination. He talked of bright lights, almond-eyed creatures, physical and mental tests. He was clever, my Adam, for seven.

Now he's gone, leaving emptiness and a vast crop circle in the garden.

Susan Wright
Worthing

What's New in 3002

Evelyn ate her replicated apple. The medicine, genetically grown into it, protected her from all disease except snake bites.

She lived with Adam, he fancied her, she loved him but he fancied Venus and Lara too. What a snake.

He left her to die with her heart full of venom.

MARGARET ANGELA BALSOM
Dulverton

It's All in the Genes

The Witchfinder General, uncovering a third nipple on Winifred, Megan's ancestor, tested her by the infallible float or drown method. Due to Winifred's irrepressible survival instinct she was proved a witch and barbecued before a crowd of righteous neighbours. Spookily, centuries later, Megan entertained spectators with her breathtaking synchronised swimming.

K. READ
Romsey

Careless Talk Costs Lives

The year is 3001. Persons using more than
5 words per day to be executed due to lack of
oxygen. (Population 10 zillion and rising.)

'Will you marry me, my darling?' He is
marched away. Defending barrister very careful
in choice of words. No more noise pollution.
Peace on Earth.

CATHERINE WARRELL
London SE9

Commended

Of the Earth

The Deleterious Effect of Man on his Environment

Somewhere in the South American jungle,
it was said, there lived a plant which ate people.
Many searched for it, and were never seen again.
Others went to find them, but they too
disappeared. Eventually, everyone gave up and
forgot about it, and the plant died through lack
of nourishment.

JOHN RAY
London SE12

Destiny . . .

'One day, son, all this will be yours!' Daniel
winced at his father's boast and glanced in
dismay at the shippons and milking parlour.

The 'City' and mega-deals beckoned.

Men from the 'Ministry'; then a convoy.
Men in khaki. Culling. Suffocating pyres. Adult
tears; adolescent smiles and propitious relief.

RALPH OWENS
Abergele

Commended

It's a Mug's Game

I am so ashamed and I pray no-one can see me.
The world is sleeping behind closed shutters.
I tiptoe through the gardens where the grass is
damp from the overnight sprinklers. The warm
air promises another lazy day by the pool.
There! I've done it. Beach towels in place!

MARILYN KANES
London SE22

Self-destruction

He loved the place for its freshness, its quiet
isolation: a star-step from the spinning world.
He shared his treasure with a friend. His friend
liked it too and built a house there. A road was
made to the house and strangers followed it.
They stayed. His star went out.

J. M. POTTER
Blundellsands

Olsztyn

We were neighbours, friends. He so fair, me so dark. We shared the clear delights of vodka, the uncomfortable mystery of girls.

War came. Home was the rank mulch of the forest. Shared fear.

Then soldiers wiped away the mud. Blue eyes saw blue. I joined my family in separation.

LYNDA BAILEY
Warsaw, Poland

Commended

War – A Saga of Four Generations

He saw violence close up. Exhausted, bloody, fractured, a forsaken island of pain.

His son saw war airborne. Dominating. Pouring cataracts of annihilation, sickened, crying.

His grandson fought great battles. Acquisitions, mergers, international ventures, bankruptcy. Heart attack.

His great-grandson fights endlessly. Bureaucracy, red tape, BSE, foot and mouth, MAFF.

J. L. GRAHAM
Portland

Press Release

At a Meeting held between Nature (in the Chair), Earth, Air, Water and Fire, at which the continuing negative impact of man on their future was discussed, it was agreed that direct intervention by them was not called for as man was making satisfactory progress towards early self-destruction and extinction.

H. F. COPPINI
Sliema, Malta

Commended

Life in Death

The early Earth, storm-torn, an early ocean:
An ocean sterile, long before life evolved.
An alien Spaceman landed, lost – light years
from civilization – now stranded on this lifeless
inhospitable planet. Eventually, he flung himself
into the barren seas to drown.
From his decaying body, life was born,
complexity began.

BRIAN ALDISS

Commissioned Story

Some of Us Are Going Places, Some Aren't

The slug in the salt ring stretched out its neck. It watched the boy's big shoe heel on the other side of the white powder ridge as he turned, cackling, and ran off for his tea. The slug peered round, cocked its tentacles and considered the options.

Which were limited.

JULIE DYE
Derby

Russia Revisited

Poor and huddled, she had reached America full
of hope, settled, her three children prospered.
Years later, a great-granddaughter from Topeka,
Kansas, intrepid though roundly obese,
journeyed back to Saratov. There, in her
crumpled shell suit, with dreams of ancestral
links forgotten, she searched vainly for a
restroom.

DIANA TURNER
London W1

Highly Commended

The Day the Circus Came to Clonakilty

The elephant entered the hotel dining-room at breakfast time. We stopped eating, nonchalantly prospecting alternative escape routes: none. Her keeper laughed, ordering her back into the lobby. Up the stairs? The hotelier paled. She departed, extracting a cabbage delicately with her trunk from a parked car. Only congealed bacon remained.

MARGERY FORESTER
Axminster

Pigeon Food

Two pigeons in Trafalgar Square.

With tourism down, an uncaring government and a serious shortage of seeds, they flew to Venice.

Settling in sunny St Mark's they gorged on garlic-encrusted ciabatta and crispy pieces of pizza.

Asked what was best about their move, they cooed in unison . . . 'No cars!'

ANITA BARDHAN-ROY
Staines

The Agoraphobic Man Finds Peace Within New Walls

Comfortably numb inside the train, he watches.
He recognises her fear as a mirror of his own,
'Why are you troubled?' Claustrophobia.
  Since they are both heading nowhere they
travel together and build their home in a
clearing and live happily in leaf topped rooms
of just the right size.

OMAR MAJEED
Hereford

Destruction

Trees whispered telling untold tales, a spring
bubbled vibrantly, birds sang their beautiful
songs and flowers bloomed in the sunset. The sky
flared orange and countless colours of sunset
fire. A breeze gently cooled the summer air.
A car materialized leaving a cigarette.
Fire sprang up obliterating peace forever.

TANYA MILLER (aged 11)
Bromley

'Old Disease – Old Remedy!'

I, the eldest son from a family of farmers.
My prize herd of Friesians – the envy of all.
I bought adjoining farms.
Our children went off to boarding school.
We planned our retirement.
Foot and Mouth arrived – bonfires lit the night.
The Bank Manager called.
I bought a new rope!

JAMES DAVID BERRY
Poulton-le-Fylde

Commended

Tragedy

The Baby

She asked him to hold the baby a minute and didn't return. Birds cried in the dusk. But it's not my child, he thought, I hardly know the woman. The writhings in his lap felt strange. Soon the baby lay still. Blue lights revolved outside. A policeman entered, with handcuffs.

BLAKE MORRISON

Commissioned Story

The Author

In the beginning was the word. The word
became a novel and the novel a film. Success
brought fame, wealth, women and trouble.
Out of his depth, waving . . . and drowning.
They dragged the author from the Hollywood
pool, bloody tracks glistening on the tiles.
His obituary had the last word.

Lynfa Landauer
Redhill

Flood Tide

Gulls cried overhead as James and Dad walked over a flat, damp sand. Neither noticed the turned tide rushing in from an unseen horizon.

'It's been a good day,' choked Dad, trying to sound cheerful as swirling water engulfed them. James just cried his young salt tears as gulls wheeled overhead.

RAYMOND PITT
Freshwater

From a View to a Kill

The task was formidable.
There would be only one chance.
The car slowly came into his view.
The victim's image was mirrored in the
        telescopic sight.
Gosh she really was beautiful.
He gently squeezed the trigger and at that exact
        moment
The President leaned across to speak to his wife.

ALAN S. DONEY
Stretford

Commended

Prizes for Wine and Wisdom

George couldn't understand why his team was so cross. He'd come because they were shorthanded.

'But I knew what "corduroy" meant!'

'Yes, and you recognised Whistler's Mother, laminaria, wild silk and leucojum.'

'Well?'

'You've ruined our collection, unbroken for twenty sessions.'

'Collection?'

'Wooden spoons, dated. We always come bottom, dimwit!'

MARGARET DUNN
Rainham

Da Capo

The Godfather, secretly coveting a henchman's wife, summoned his captains.

'We have a tout. Waste him – soonest. In his Sardinian villa. Gun from local contact . . . omertà assured.'

Hitman despatched.

Three days later, the call.

'Done. Poolside job.'

'Witnesses?'

'None.'

The Godfather smiled.

'Oh – just the wife . . . but stiffed her too.'

CHRISTOPHER PELLY
Parkstone

The Wood for the Trees

He had to escape,
break out of the forest –
to reach Griselda,
ever patient, now imprisoned,
for which he blamed himself.
He hacked at branches,
slashed the undergrowth,
fought trolls and wolves.
Still no escape.
He slept, exhausted.
Griselda appeared, then gently said,
'The forest, love, is in your head.'

PATRICK DRYSDALE
Abingdon

A Woman's Intuition Is Always Right

He was always working late or away for days.

Signs of an affair.

She had done a car maintenance course, his suggestion.

She knew how to 'fix' the brakes.

He leaves next morning.

Noon, flowers arrive, card reads:

'Surprise, surprise, darling. Dream House finished.'

1 o'clock News, fatal car crash.

MRS MAUREEN MASON
Ashington

If an Infinite Number of Monkeys . . .

They'd been typing for aeons. God read, and a frown creased the Celestial Brow.

'THE TRAGICAL HISTORY . . .'

The Eyebrows lifted as the ape continued:

'. . . OF HAMLET, PRINCE . . .'

One hairy finger scratched one simian head.

'. . . OF . . .'

God held His Breath . . .

'. . . GSJKEOTHZ.'

'Take your time,' He murmured. 'Infinity hasn't even begun yet.'

MICHAEL CARVER
Flushing

Commended

74

Reality Can Be Painful

Lost love found on Radio Two e-mail made
contact – telephone calls followed – meeting
arranged under the clock at Waterloo – just like
in 1942.

Memory plays tricks – years have not been kind
– attractive uniforms long gone – too much water
under the bridge – seeing you again has been
pleasant – but goodbye!

NATALIE WINETROUBE
Elloughton

The Battle of Burnham Green

We're pinned down by sniper fire. Someone talked – we've been betrayed.

If we don't move now we'll be cut off and surrounded.

Sergeant Thomas gives the signal. Bayonets at the ready, we charge the enemy. Over the sound of gunfire I hear a distant voice cry,

'John! Your tea's ready.'

PAUL SNOOK-BROWN
Easterton

Life, After-Life (A True Story)

Car-struck, drifting beneath consciousness.
Monitors roared and bleeped his response to
    endearments.
We left in shocked complaisance, unendurable
    grief,
hoping love would heal.
Next night, his spirit stood nearby. I cried,
'Go . . . stay, you choose. We will always love you.'
He woke next day, and our new lives began.

Christine Fiona Baker
Higher Woodsford

Pen Friends

She was 15 when they took the baby. She wrote every week, 18 years of letters to the adoption people. When she was 33, Stevie walked in, his dead father's spit. He had read 938 letters in two weeks. He'd come to say he didn't want to be in touch.

JUDY DELIN
Dunblane

If You Want a Very Nice Time Just Give This Number a Call

Buster eagerly dialled Babylon 6 87 87, 'Hello,' the female voice answered. 'Hhhello,' Buster stuttered. 'I sssaw your number in the phone box and' – 'Buster, is that you?' the voice interrupted. 'Mmiranda!?' 'Yes. Oh God, please don't tell Mum.' 'But . . .' 'Please?' 'OK. I wwwon't.' 'Thanks. I owe you.' 'Yeah. Bbbye.'

FELICE NEALS
London N1

End of Battle

Maltman moved weakly.

'It's dammed 'ot. Fever,' he said and fell back.

'The Kaffirs – are the barricades 'olding? – Smuts will be 'ere soon.'

His aide went to the window. This Jamaican nurse, this old man dying. Outside a January London; snow falling heavily; distant gunfire in the night.

ROY HEATH
Pulborough

Highly Commended

Yes, It Certainly Moved All Right

They had a new life together. So much in love.

They revelled in the hot climate.

Every day was for living and loving.

'I love you passionately, darling.'

'Then make love to me passionately.'

'Darling, did you feel the earth move?'

Next day their bodies were recovered from the rubble.

D. F. JOHN
Hingham

Commended

Leave-taking

He took her hand. She took his money.

He took a lover.

She took exception. He took leave of his senses. She took advice. He took fright.

She took him to the cleaner's. He took to drink.

She took a holiday.

He took his life.

She took up ballroom dancing.

SUSIE BAMFORTH
Durweston

Commended

He Who Laughs Last

He used to laugh at my mock-crocodile-skin shoes and matching handbag. 'Philistine,' he called me. Then he left me to travel the world. The last thing I heard was that a crocodile had eaten him. They found only his shoes, washed up on the bank of a river.

GILLIAN PARKER
Wokingham

A Political Diary

1992
Me: 17,851 votes.
Vile McCluskey: 21,243 votes.
Margaret asks me to put up the lounge shelves.

1997
Me: 20,215.
Wretched McCluskey: 20,673.
Poised for victory! Margaret says *please* put up the shelves.

2001
Me: 20,420.
McCluskey: 20,421
Margaret voted for McCluskey. Says *that'll* teach me to ignore her.
Cow.

DAN WICKSMAN
Cambridge

Travelling

Bermuda Bus Ride

It arrives at the pink and blue pole. It is pink and blue itself. Its driver, Mrs Mason, greets us.

It takes us past pink and blue houses, past pink sands and turquoise blue seas. At the final pink and blue pole, we thank Mrs Mason.

You're welcome, she says.

DIANA BISHOP
Doune

Runner-up

Gifts of the Magi
6th January 2001

E mail to Melchior, Balthazar, Caspar: Magi.

Dear Mr Magi,

Re your esteemed order

Due to unforeseen circumstances substitution of items inevitable

For gold: reprocessed plutonium (better value)

frankincense: 500 joss sticks (very prayerful)

myrhh: 10 tubs excellent quality lanolin

All goods gift wrapped

www.Bannerjeeexoticsupplies.com.calcutta.

ANN WICKHAM
Westcott

Highly Commended

Survivor

At our age we didn't expect to fall in love again.
We chose the Greek islands for our honeymoon.
As the ferry capsized, he helped me with the
life jacket then held me tight. A year into our
marriage, when he hugs me, I feel only the fear
of drowning.

DEBORAH SEYMAN
London N1

Commended

Theorem

I
fell in
love, married,
and then honeymooned
in Egypt, where I realised I had
made a mistake. I fled the land of pyramids
and, eventually, met a mathematician who was
fascinated by Pythagoras and triangular numbers. Last
year he died and I felt free at last of geometrical arrangements.

MIRANDA STONOR
London SW12

Commended

The Road to Delphi

Once sleepless babe, stranger to tenderness,
then wild shunned girl reading behind
frightened eyes banal destinies, later
unpartnered seer in stony wilderness she divined
with cold ecstasy in burning entrails eternal
cycles of hatred and revenge, until, sibilant
crone, she foresaw in wreathed smoke her own
pyre and ineluctable reincarnation.

ANGELA PULLIN
Kettlebaston

The Traveller

He was warm and safe but outside beckoned.
It was time. Forces beyond his control propelled
him forward. Lungs bursting, limbs aching,
distant noises grew louder as he struggled to
the surface. Light hit his face and, gasping for
breath, he let out a strangled cry.

'Congratulations, it's a boy!'

JO FORD
Chelmsford

Your Whole Future – Behind You

'Well Ian,' Valdez began, 'how do you like Puerto Rico now – eh?' The tape over my mouth made speech impossible. 'Oh come now, you must have enjoyed the scenery as much as you apparently enjoyed my wife?' His smile crumbled as he fell forward. '*Ex*-wife,' Maria hissed, withdrawing the dagger.

ROBIN WILLIAMS
Penarth

Travelling with Botticelli: A Journey of Discovery from Intellect to Senses

The voyage took me by storm.

I was cracking the enigma of *Primavera*,
when suddenly I *became* Chloris – forgiving
Zephyrus' rape, my mouth spewing flowers;
reconciling fecund Venus with Mercury's sword.
Flora subsumed me. As searching gave way
to acceptance, Graces danced in a pattern
of triangles.

I had arrived.

COLIN WILCOCKSON
Cambridge

A Holiday of a Lifetime

'Welcome aboard this two-hour flight to the sun,' the captain announced.

'There is a choice of chicken or beef,' said the stewardess, then screamed at Malcolm, 'please would your turn off that mobile.'

'We have an emergency, adopt the brace position, brace, sh . . .'

The black box revealed the story.

DEREK TAYLOR
Morwenstow

Distillation of a Life

Thirteen years ago, her first sight of Africa.

Thirteen years of toil, exhilaration and heartbreak.

Today, the dusty heat of a colonial railway station. Clasped hands, white on black. Deep yearning and sorrow at what both know is a final parting.

Ahead, years of bitter-sweet longing for this life.

TIM MEAKIN
London E1

Key to the Highway

Groom loved roadster. On honeymoon drive to
Salamanca bride realised error. They sipped
coffee in Plaza Mayor. He asked if she felt free.
She smiled and rose and wandered. High heat:
sunlight and shadow. He lost her and his car-key.
She had the wind in her hair. She felt free.

WYNN WHELDON
London N6

Journeys

'Although I love you,' he declared, 'I must travel; when I return, we will marry.' From beyond the oceans and the far mountains he sent her warm words and rich gifts. On his return she told him: 'I married the chap next door; his presence meant more than your presents.'

BRIAN CROOK
Lambourn

Nothing Lasts Forever

The Seeker searched the desert dunes, fluid wind-sculpted mountains, seeking something permanent in impermanence.

He scanned the changing horizons.
He consulted tent-living desert nomads.
They puzzled, shrugged, and moved on.

Lying fatigued on the shifting sand, he faced the sky, the infinite void. Then he understood: Only nothing lasts forever.

DIANE WILLIAMS
Bridgend

The Journey

She was searching, and decided to go on a
journey. So she prepared, planned, packed, and
so began. The drive was long, but she stopped –
for food, drink, and petrol. On she went, into the
evening, on into the dark, still more travelling.
At last she'd arrived, and discovered – herself.

Susan Blake
Moulton Leys

The Unbearable Lightness of Being Down and Out in Greece Contemplating the Meaning of Lettuce

Another ripple of calm blue sea lapped the pebble-dashed shore. Paradise had dealt a cruel blow to Fiona.

Dreams of speed and overwhelming power to feed her addiction were dashed. Her adrenaline withdrawal as predictable as the doldrums.

'Why?' she asked.

'It's just Kos,' answered the bronzed Brad-Pitt-stomached windsurfing instructor.

FIONA LEWINS
London SW4

Crane

Fledgling romance at work, an origami paper
shop. Unsigned letter arrives, a warning.
A fireplace. Letter is burnt. Misunderstanding.
Years pass. An encounter at Heathrow. Malta.
Walking on warm volcanic stone, hands linked.
Love? Love! Creased bed sheets. Squid.
Anaphylactic shock. Helicopter rescue. Recovery.
Origami bird in flight. Kiss. Oh.

CAROL SHIELDS

Commissioned Story

Horror

Fish and Chips

Broken wipers had him braking at eighty
when his windscreen was hit by wrapped fish
    and chips –
cars up his arse and horns in his head –
lights coming on like lights in a theatre
when the wrapper split like a caterpillar skin
slapping cod and batter between him and
    eternity

MIRIAM OBREY
Ditton Priors

His Most Difficult Case

'While the motive for the third murder is still opaque to me,' said the Cardinal quietly, 'I am now sure that the stolen codex was in fact a forgery; that the Major was an impostor; that Lady Winteringham had more than one accomplice; and that my son is still alive.'

JOHN LANCHESTER

Commissioned Story

The Hair

The hair began appearing after his father died, unmourned: in combs; behind the glass of old photos; floating down from the loft.

And one night matted in his throat.

He climbed the stairs.

In the corner of the attic a skeleton wore the lopsided wig his mother had disappeared in.

SIMON MILES
London E15

Too Much Agatha Christie, or An Inspector Calls

He was pathetically easy to take. His overweening vanity made such a virtue of habit. The lobotomy was crude but very effective. He sat there, his moustaches awry. I waved the filled jam-jar in front of his unseeing green eyes. 'What about your precious little grey cells now, Moosier Poirot?'

CHARLES JOHNSTON
London SE27

A Born Loser

She recognised the writing on the envelope immediately. The gipsy had warned her that she had no future with this man, yet here he was – five lonely years after their last meeting – begging her to join him in New York.

She was blissfully happy as she stepped aboard the *Titanic*.

JEAN PRESSLING
Upminster

Able Was I Ere I Saw Elba

'De Montholon, help me to return to France and I will reward you,' said Napoleon.

'Highness, I work daily to bring that about,' murmured his jailer.

'I shall return in glory!' roared Napoleon, his eyes blazing.

'You will return in a coffin,' thought de Montholon as he poured more wine.

TERESA BROWN
Bishop's Stortford

Civility, Civic Virtue and the Deontology of Crime

August scorcher. Packed bus. Crazy driver.
Pregnant woman standing. Nice man tells yob to
yield priority seat. Scuffle ends at police station.
Nice man gets detained. He's wanted for a grisly
murder. Trying to make up for lost time, driver
crashes the bus into a tree. Pregnant woman
gets killed.

NIKOLA NAYDENOV
London SW18

The Norseman Cometh

The invasion of Yorkshire had been hard and
Thorfinn and his Vikings were resting, when he
was accosted by Agnes, a local lass:

'Finished with the pillaging, ducky?' she asked.

Thorfinn opened his eyes.

'Yes. Why do you ask?'

'The girls would like to know what time the
raping starts.'

E. I. MEDCALF
Cheadle

Commended

No Sweat?

'Either her waterproof leaks or she perspires.'
   'I will find out, James.'
   On an equatorial afternoon she slumbered
near my Sister. Taking Henry, our tiny
dehydrating hamster, on his constitutional
I gazed down into her voluptuous cavernous
cleavage and dropped Henry in.
   'What happened?' demanded James.
   'Very sad: Henry drowned.'

TOM MURPHY
Christchurch

Just Desserts?

Sisters, we had similar tastes in everything but
him. 'He's a dish,' you said and married him.
I thought him unsavoury.
   He battered you, saying,
    'Only death do us part.'
In a jam, you called.
   Our last course? . . .
                A sticky end.
                    Death by chocolate.
   Afterwards, we agreed, he was delicious.

Vanessa Galvin
Rochester

A Bird in the Hand

Shielding his eyes, he searches the heavens.
White wings against blue sky!
   A target!
   Airgun in his hand. Excitement in his chest.
   He fires. It falls.
   He runs. Part of the sky is his!
   But arriving finds only disappointment lying in
the gutter, with the blood, feathers and broken
harp.

VANESSA GALVIN
Rochester

Filthy Lucre

'Take the bleedin' money,' he shrieked,
plummeting to a watery death.

She caught the bag, stuffed with bloodstained
notes.

Back in her flat she washed them, selecting
'Heavily stained delicates'.

Knock, knock. They burst in. 'She's laundered
it for us.'

She spun round then shrank but they blew her
away.

Jo Griffiths
Rhiwbina

Dark Plots in the Tool-Shed

'This time,' whispered the hedge-trimmer,
'we finish him, me and Step-ladder,
I shock him . . . Ladder drops him . . . splatt.'
'Nooo . . .' Dutch-hoe quavered.
'Shut it,' Spade snarled. 'Yesterday
he crippled Lady-fork. DO IT!'

'You nearly killed yourself this time,'
        the woman said.
'Bloody . . .' He hesitated . . .
'GO ON!', she hissed, 'blame your tools.'

DENNIS ENTICOTT
Wimborne

Commended

Incorrect Punctuation

As Eng Lit Prof, he wooed with words: beautiful,
bountiful. She bloomed. Exclamation mark.

Made poetry together, wallowed in superlatives
and sticky love stanzas. In parenthesis.

Marriage life sentence spared no space for
student subclauses. Semicolon.

Sorry . . . Ellipsis.

Pre-suicide poem, her best work ever,
he published. Full stop.

New paragraph.

MAGGIE INNES
London SE12

A Different Spring

The air seemed thick, the vegetation tasted different this spring.

The little creature instinctively darted, started, but there was no rustling behind her, no swooping above; no predators.

She ate, fattened and bore two live young and seven dead, following her protracted gestation.

All was different after the nuclear winter.

ANNE DAWSON
London SE12

The Invasion of the Nightmare Land

One day I woke up from a terrible dream. Then the monster jumped out of the bed . . . arrgh . . . I ran down the stairs as fast as I could. Finally I escaped the monster but then I saw a strange man with sharp-blooded razor claws.

MARCUS QUINN (aged 7)
Birmingham

Progress

'Sikh and Ye Shall Find' (or: Those Who Adapt, Survive)

Vijay arrived, penniless. Terrace windows announced 'No blacks'. Relatives squeezed him in. Neighbours sprayed 'fresh air' over the fence, muttering 'Stinking Pakis'.

Factory air soiled white turbans. He wore black. Beards? Forbidden. He shaved. Now Vijay's own factory announces 'No vacancies'. His Rolls patrols terraced streets, spraying windows with rainwater.

HELEN YENDALL
Coleshill

Lifestyle

A young hippie couple lived in a house in the woods, worshipped nature, scorned the conventions. Peaceful anarchists, they rejected materialism. They said to their two children, 'We are going out for the day – you can look after yourselves.'

The children whispered to each other, 'We can have a bath!'

ROSEMARY FITCH
Godalming

Donna e Mobile

'This is a highly covetous area,' said the estate agent. Donna, recently divorced, loved the electric gates. 'There's a panic button in the master bedroom,' he boasted. Eventually, though, she decided it wasn't big enough for her gargantuan needs. His cold hand grasped hers. 'You could always *extend*,' he urged.

HELEN SIMPSON

Commissioned Story

Consumer's Lot

He bought the thing he didn't need, with money
he didn't have, from someone he didn't know.
It had been designed by someone he hadn't
heard of. It was built by someone who didn't
care, in a country he'd never been to. He got it
home and it didn't work.

KEVIN LEVELL
Lyne

Commended

Animal Rights – Reality Bites

The laboratory blazed. We ran gleefully, justified into the night.

Years later and half a world away my young daughter screamed. The Taipan slid away from the pool.

Shock!

Panic!

But help soon arrived. An injection given – she would survive!

'Great serum,' the paramedic exclaimed, 'developed in England you know!'

IAN BENNETT
Buckden

What Would You Do if You Could Travel Back in Time?

The murders were universally condemned. Governments from around the world expressed outrage. There could be no justification. The killer was executed and civilisation applauded the resolute stand against terrorism. The tragic deaths, it was agreed, of Chancellor Hitler and his chiefs of staff, were a great loss to the nation.

JOHN FOSKETT
Holmes Chapel

Devolution

An eye stalk, developed between adjacent ice ages, plopped up out of the ooze. Its owner surveyed the gently sloping shore and imagined the ascent. It would need legs, a central nervous system and eventually some kind of rudimentary dress sense. On the whole, it was just too much bother.

MICHAEL CORLETT
Thame

Highly Commended

The Wages of Spin

He picked up the phone with a cheery: 'How can I mislead you?'

Would his client resign, I demanded angrily. I had the Belize tapes – no room for doubt.

'Your station's biggest advertiser? They won't run it,' he laughed. 'Trust me, I'm a PR man.'

My tape was still running.

ROGER CARROLL
New Malden

Will Pollution of Land, Sea and Sky End Life on Our Planet?

The giant leatherback turtle had swum across the oceans of the world ten times in his 100 years of life. Calm or storm, feast or famine, day or night, summer or winter he circumnavigated the globe, serene, powerful, healthy – his diet floating, pulsing jellyfish, his death a plastic bag.

P. GRIFFITHS
Wick

Regular Meetings

At our first meeting he arrived on all fours, covered in hair. Next time he walked upright, carrying a spear. Last time: mounted, wearing cotton.

Today he arrived by boat, trailing noxious fumes.

For his camera I smile my iguana smile but secretly think that we will not meet again.

NIGEL LODGE
Great Gransden

First Prize

Weaving Ways

At Oxford, friends were surprised at her comprehensive school background. Always interested in justice, she went on to become a brilliant barrister, winning many high-profile cases. Then politics beckoned. Now an ambitious MP, she reflected on how her life was shaped: her mother was a witch and so was she.

E. A. DINSDALE
Camberley

The Diplomat

He had James his driver and lover
But needed a wife to advance his career.

She, a widow, needed security and
Longed for a companion.

They married according to convention,
Conformed to social values and were content.

He with his driver and lover
And she with her lover, his driver.

ANNETTE WHITMORE
St Neots

Trouble with Beanstalks

Once Upon a Time
    'Green fingers, Jack?'
    'No. It's a genetically modified bean.'

Later the Same Day
    'Where's Jack?'
    'Gone to test his recurring acrophobia
problem.'

Even Later
    'That's a fine axe, Jack, but will MAFF let you
cut it down?'
    'Unlikely. But hopefully it'll solve my recent
gigantophobia difficulty!'

ANDREW LEWIS
Woking

Commended

Words of Worth

The poet sought inspiration in the Lakeland mists.

One day as he trudged up and down the hills, alone amongst the clouds, he suddenly came upon thousands of yellow dandelions drooping in the drizzle.

'Aha,' he mused, 'with a little poetic licence this could be the start of something big.'

EMMA FOURACRE
Bearsted

Commended

Pour Encourager les Autres

The old pals met again, many years after the Somme offensive. 'Fred! You were court-martialled. We were told you'd been executed. For cowardice, they said!'

'I changed places with my guard,' Fred replied.

'But how?'

'He wanted it so. He could not endure the front again. Who's the coward?'

PATRICK O'CONNOR
Stevenage

Commended

Religion

Fallen Fruit

Wasps collect under the Tree. Eve scratches her belly, nudging the pulp with her toe.

'We did the right thing?'

Adam yawns, twisting lilies from their stems. Eve looks away and back again.

'You seen God lately?'

The lily scent fades, Adam struggles to remember. He shrugs,

'Not for ages.'

R. GARNER
Basford

Commended

La Plus ça Change

The parishoner wept. 'My wife's gone, I'm unemployed, and my son's unjustly imprisoned.'

The priest nodded sagely. 'It will pass,' he said, gently.

Months later, the man bounced joyfully into church.

'My wife's back, my son's out, I'm earning bucket-loads.'

The priest nodded sagely. 'It will pass,' he said gently.

Andrew Madden
London N22

Commended

Collected Mini-Sagas

Married woman elopes with army officer, is disillusioned and dies. Bored French housewife seeks romantic adventure, is disillusioned and dies. Witty girl gets richer husband than her nice sister. God rids luckless governess of her rich boyfriend's mad wife. French bloke, looking back, blames girl trouble on his mother.

RACHEL CUSK

Commissioned Story

The One True God

A priest and a rabbi were out walking, arguing theology.

'Why argue?' shrugged the rabbi. 'Look. God is like those two trees.'

And he stode into the park, pointing:

'Describe them, please!'

'Those trees? Very well . . . um . . . they're standing side by side –'

'Fool! *One is plainly standing behind the other!*'

SIMON HEYWOOD
Pitsmoor

Bringers of Light

In the beginning, darkness.

First light brought artless tyrants and man, blinking at new earth. He fought the blackness of sleep, straightening himself across frontiers. The imaginings of lifetimes encrusted her with luminous warmth.

And earth ungrateful, propelled him to new darknesses, conscious the circle must close, in the end.

NEIL G. HENDRY
Gourock

Creation's Paradox

Almighty God was ambivalent. Though fascinating, formative and fearsome, dinosaurs did not reflect him. Something in my image! Adam was born; then emerged Eve.

Naturally, but unconscionably, flesh succumbed.

So God invented religion from original sin. But this led to abandoning his Eden scheme. Christianity blossomed – without advancing animal rights.

DR PAUL KEARNS
Manchester

The Annunciation

When Mary awoke Gabriel was no longer there.
His words had wowed her. The mystery of his
feathery presence had brought the blood to her
cheeks and a longing to her womb. She was now
with child. Outside the window the blue-trunked
cypress trembled. Twenty centuries' troubles
lay ahead.

David J. K. Evans
Exeter

God Is an Englishman, or What Really Occurred in the Garden of Eden

Adam delved; Eve span; the snake lurked. Bliss. Then Eve got a yen for apples and God went bananas. Adam cursed Eve, Eve blamed the snake, God blamed everyone and the snake cursed his luck. God toyed with mercy, then decided, foreknowingly: 'This will make a great subject for Milton.'

IAIN COLLEY
Lancaster

The Secret

'Motherhood? Then you'll need a man.'

'A man?'

'He'll be sexy, strong; a companion.'

'Great! Drawbacks?'

'Aggression, dominance, ego, so you must let him believe he came first, not yourself.'

'What!'

'Sorry, but to succeed, it is essential we keep that bit our secret, Eve, woman to woman,' said God.

JILL DAVIES
Fernhurst

Some Eccentricities

Hard Times

No-one met Lizzie's train.

Too old to carry her cases, she found a porter within the hour. A sullen cabbie left her trembling on the guesthouse steps. Fish fingers and sleeplessness burnt peeling walls and sharp springs on her mind.

'Holidays were such fun when We were Queen,' she murmured.

MICHAEL NIXON
Penuwch

The Revenge of Special Agent Demalio

Midnight. He waited, weapon firmly clenched. 'He will return,' he thought, yawning. He was sick of these sleepless nights.

A sudden noise and he raised his hand. The noise became louder. It was now or never. Wham!

'Take that!' he yelled. Smack! He sighed in relief.

Mission accomplished. Mosquito dead.

BEVAN FRANK
London NW11

Daisy and Delia Go Shopping

'Wan' um,' said Daisy, jabbing the catalogue.
Her aim was off; so Delia focused on a thermos.
'We never have picnics, darling.' Difficult words
made Daisy shout. 'Summatheese!' Jab, Jab.
Delia stared, astonished. 'Fairy Wings? Why?'
'To go quietly,' Daisy said, enunciating
meticulously.

   'Oh, Mum,' sighed Delia, 'time for tea.'

JANE CUNNINGHAM
London SE13

Highly Commended

Anger Management

Tom's Dad met *her* at the drama group.

When he moved in with her, Mum was crushed. Tom didn't speak to him for three years, until his breakdown. Then he phoned.

'Tom?? Is that you?'

'Come and get me Dad . . .'

'Where are you?'

'The Blackwall Tunnel . . . I need a tow.'

Steve Chambers
Newcastle upon Tyne

Can Can Comeback

Contemptuous, wardens from the old age home sneered: 'Try charity shops.'

Fanny did. Travelling country wide by coach, demolishing her meagre income collecting raunchy French knickers.

They scoffed: 'Bonkers.'

Fanny died. The home was bequeathed her treasured lingerie collection.

Sid, her favourite driver, unwound in Corfu on his windfall legacy.

MARTINE COULTER
Warwick

On the Importance of Lateral Thinking When Planning the Destruction of Maiden-Eating Dragons

A large, scaly dragon had been devouring maidens at an unsustainable rate. It had repelled many attempts on its life by brave young knights.

George, unskilled in the arts of broadsword and lance, hit upon the solution. He ravished every maiden for ten miles around.

The dragon starved to death.

P. J. CHANDLER
Totnes

Lighting Man

'Stand in the light.' The man bellowed from the auditorium.

He'd fought in Vietnam hence the attitude.

'A hard bastard,' Lofty said.

Lofty knew. They'd argued one night on the crew bus. He'd beaten Lofty black blue and amber. The lighting man covered me in colours and stood in the darkness.

RAY DAVIES

Commissioned Story

The Last Post

Job Description.   Sub-postmistress.

Peace suddenly shattered, balaclava head yelled, 'Give us the money.'

I crouched down. Screen broken, glass shards everywhere. Male assistant and Alsatian hide.

Shots fired. Wish I was thinner, lessen the odds. *Ouch.*

Assistant received £300 bravery award.

New Job Description.   Ghost.
Duty.   To haunt chicken-livered assistant.

JEAN LOUGHREY
Fulmodeston

Money or Your Life

The frail old lady trembled as she stared at the barrel of the handgun. Her legs were weak and she felt sick.

His dark eyes glared hard at her.

'Hand over all your money.'

The cold steel gun waved menacingly.

'I will,' he stammered as he emptied his trouser pockets.

BERYL LUCY
Gorton

First Interview

'Come!' from behind a newspaper.

'I'm Emily.' The last cigarette still sharp in her mouth.

'I know. Surprise me!'

'Excuse me?'

'Surprise me!'

The newspaper stayed up, fingers at either end. She watched herself reach the lighter across the desk. Watched as flames went like a cat up a curtain.

PAUL BLANEY
London N5

Highly Commended

The Lion and the Lamb

The lion lay down with the lamb.
'He's such a vile vulgarian,'
Said Lamb. 'I hate him. Damn!
Pity I'm a vegetarian
Or else I'd eat him whole,
This big fat jungle cat!'
Almost beyond control
And knowing little fear,
He bit the lion's ear.
The lion pounced. That's that!

BRIAN ALDISS

Commissioned Story

Double the Trouble

Albert Drizzleworth was a loss adjuster and also a bigamist, with one family in Ealing and another in Ecuador. Unaccountably Albert disappeared, but wrote to his wives, telling each about the other.

They met and decided, with Albert gone, to gain a fresh husband and perversely chose Albert's twin brother.

Nicholas King
Bristol

Other Lives

Even on the mountain, little children chased
them, one hand holding a flower, the other
extended, cupped.

'Bloody beggars,' he grumbled.

One, of course, was lame, came last. She
dropped a coin into that tiny hand and shocked,
felt calloused, work-hardened, torn skin.

She took the flower and kissed it.

SHELAGH MOORHOUSE
London W11

A Dream So Real

Staying overnight with friends, his sleep was disturbed by a vivid dream: a thief broke in, stole everything in the flat – then carefully replaced every single item with an exact replica.

'It felt so real,' he told his friends in the morning.

Horrified, uncomprehending, they replied, 'But who are you?'

PATRICK FORSYTH
Maldon

Highly Commended

~~Spring Summer~~
~~Autumn~~ Winter Cleaning

My house looks as though it's been hit by a bomb.
Since I'm hopeless at organising, I bought a
book: *Key to organising your life*. I felt so proud.

I started with the bookcase. Five minutes later,
I sat back, wide-eyed in disbelief.

I'd bought the same book last year.

RACHAEL GARDNER
London SW12

Commended

Age – and After

Knock Knock

'Who is it?'

'Anna. Meals-on-Wheels.'

''Bout time. I'll get the chain. Thought yer name was Agnes.'

'Take care, there's a conman about pretending he's from the Water Board.'

'I'm old, not daft.'

* * *

'Who is it?'

'Water Board.'

''Bout time. I'll get the chain. Agnes said you was coming.'

PAULINE KAZI
Bexhill on Sea

Commended

Grave Matter; Stumped Out

She had stroked the gnarled, stooping apple tree
blocking their path, musing on shared
memories. 'Prop it up, I want burying here!'
When she was out, Bill took a chainsaw to it.
The old tree groaned, slipped and he amputated
his leg. Forlornly, she tends his grave beneath
the stump.

D. G. BARKER
Sidcup

Flashbacks

Woken by the treble of birdsong, crotchet on clean white page. Mum's voice, 'Wake up kids, it snowed last night.'

Walking the aisle. Familiar faces through fresh net lens. Him kissing me, cameras exploding.

Breast-feeding.

The doctor diagnosing cancer.

Sharp intake of disinfectant. Sinking back into soft white light.

PATIENCE AGBABI
London N5

Commended

Closure

Being born, Grace almost killed her mother, she had often been told.

All her life Grace wanted to make amends; but however she tried it was never enough.

Thirty years later, 'Help me . . .' whispered her dying mother.

Placing a pillow over the emaciated face she loved, Grace completed the circle.

MARGARET FRANCIS
Chester

The Case of the Persistent Son

'Please, please can I have a briefcase.' 'Why can't I have a briefcase?'

'All my friends have briefcases.'

Norman Adam continued to pester his parents, day in day out.

Finally exhausted, the Gordons gave in and presented their son with a briefcase with his initials boldly engraved on the front.

Derek Wine
Edgbaston

Wrong Address

Everyone had an invitation to Bob's party.
Except me. Got sympathy from friends. Some
speculation. Why? Everyone planning what to
wear. Except me. Party came. Everyone had fun.
Except me.

Neighbour came. 'Here, this came for you last
week. Sorry, I forgot.'

She was very old. Everyone understood.
Except me.

CAROL HAWES
Normandy

Relicts

Fred and Ginger were cats. Fred was a ginger cat;
Ginger was not. My husband gave them names
with many resonances. Now Fred is dead, and
so is my husband. Ginger, who was never ginger,
and I, who was a wife, remain, bewildered, in
a world where nothing makes sense.

KATHRYN PUFFETT
Cambridge

Marriage Vows

On the bed, she feels his breathing cease.
Next to his cooling warmth she remembers
seven decades of nurtured love, summer picnics,
easy laughter, moonlight dances, gentle touching,
shared baths, hardships conquered, counting wrinkles –
doing everything together. Her chest falls,
but does not rise, a lasting smile on her lips.

HEATHER FOWLER
Weston-super-Mare

Observed from a Reliant Robin

One spring day I saw them. Two ladies in matching wheelchairs.

Summer; a straw hat apiece, laughing uproariously as they bumped from kerb to kerb.

But autumn – same road – one wheelchair.

My day was saddened.

Then winter and two again – sou'westers against the weather.

I smiled my way to work.

JUDITH HAMMOND
Denmead

Runner-up

The Journey

The journey took a lifetime. Learn as you go.
No maps or rule books. The face that looks back
at me is a record of past pains and pleasures.
Who plotted my path? Was it random or design?
No questions answered. Journeys end: I go
forward into a new dimension.

MAUREEN TOYN
Holmrook

Never Let an Innocent Man Die Because of a Misunderstanding

The argument got more heated. The knife went in. Blood came out. Francis ran. Was caught, tried and hanged. Media rejoiced. Time elapsed. The argument got more heated. The knife went in. Blood came out. A man ran. Caught and tried, admits previous crimes. Francis' widow weeps in growing realisation.

MICHAEL FINDLAY
King's Lynn

Growing Young

Today, I am growing old. Who can grow when ageing? My body has shrunk, my brain functions less – slow down then breakdown.

Today, I leave with twenty others over 70 years prepared for the unknown, our rocket launches at dawn.

We will grow young on our planet in space. Goodbye!

Mrs Mitchell
Leeds

She Said No

She said no. He persuaded the jury it was no meaning yes.

Years later their paths crossed again. She unrecognisable, he with a face she'd never forget.

As she fastened his safety harness he asked was he safe? No, she said laughing.

Accidental death? asked the jury. She said yes.

EMMA BUCKLEY
London E11

Highly Commended

No Claim Bonus

Nagasaki, August 9.

    Brakes squeal, metal crumples, tempers fray. No injuries but heated words, disputed blame. Personal details are tersely exchanged.

    Each returns to his damaged motor with bruised feelings, cursing the day which had begun so well.

    Five miles above them, the super fortress has opened its bomb doors.

M. J. TAIT
Willerby

Runner-up

Love

Birthday Present

My Sixtieth Birthday. Harry's Bar. She arrived,
such elegance, youth and beauty. The head
turning made her the centre of attention.
We embraced. Finishing our drinks, we left.
Near the door a young man asked jealously,
'Why someone so young with someone so old?'
'He married my mother,' she replied.

DEREK SEAWARD
London E14

The Devoted Secretary

Each working day for twenty years she placed
a rose in the vase she had brought for his desk.
He smiled, but never spoke of it.

At his funeral his widow told her how he had
given her a rose every workday when he came
home.

She smashed the vase.

TERESA BROWN
Bishop's Stortford

Commended

Forecourt, Forethought

I loved her but could not tell her. Petrol pump attendant she was, but my Juliet. I concocted my plan. One night I drove in, filled up. I had no money. Would you accept this ring as payment – a diamond? 'Yes,' she said. I skipped out, happy, contented and engaged.

P. Spillane
Bournville

An Alphabetical, Amorous Adventure

Ardent, ambitious,
brooding boy,
Charles, confesses
desperate desire,
even erotic
fancy, for
grasping girl.

Handily, having
inherited interesting
jewels, juvenile
keeps kissing
lovely lass.

Mercenary miss,
necessarily nice!

Options occur!

Previous paramour,
quixotically questing
romance, reappears,
seeking sexual
tryst. Temptation!

Unique union!

Voracious voluptuary
weds woman.

X-it
youthful, yearning
zealot.

JOHN MARTIN
Hampton

Telephone Engaged

He walked past the street phone as it rang.
Curious, he answered. She asked for the
'Mysterious Dating Agency'. Wickedly he agreed,
chatted and took her details down. Later he
called back arranging a meeting identified by
carnations. He walked into the restaurant
whistling 'Jerusalem'. He explained during their
honeymoon.

JAMES L. YOUNG
Hunsdon

Mind the Gap

Undaunted, he hacked through thickets of
thorn, hands bleeding, to claim his bride.
A kiss awoke her from her hundred years' sleep.
But miscommunications through a century's gap
cut wounds that wouldn't heal. The night she left
him for his grandfather, he held his head in
scarred hands, and cried.

PAULINE INGALL
Betley

Footprints

Mrs Bridges and Jim woke to find unexpected snow outside their remote love nest. Tyre marks and size 10 footprints greeted Mr Bridges when he returned from London at four.

'The freezer packed up,' said Mrs Bridges. 'The repairman came.'

'Good service in this weather,' he said.

'Excellent,' she agreed.

MARGARET KNOX
Beccles

Commended

Tears for Leah

Though Larry so adored fair Leah
he never made intention clear.
She, tiring of procrastination,
found escape by emigration.

Leah rebounded onto Ted.
Heady passion and they wed.
Larry heard the news and shed
tears for 'Will you?' never said.

Decades later,
marriage bust,
Leah hunts Larry;
finds him –
dust.

CHRISTOPHER ALDERSON
Edinburgh

Tempus Fugit

He was worried.

Since his wife's death, his teenage daughter had become increasingly touchy.

But they had agreed 2.00am as the latest return time from 'clubbing'. It was now 3.30am.

He steeled himself for confrontation as the door opened.

'Dad!!' she shouted – 'I've been frantic – you're late again.'

JAMES O'CONNOR
Baltonsborough

And Yet So Far

At school, he yearned for her but never spoke.

   He studied Law in London; her tutor told her Birmingham was better for Biology.

   He handled her divorce impeccably.

   'I always fancied him,' she told his daughter at his funeral, 'I sometimes wish I'd had the nerve to tell him so.'

MARY JONES
Topsham

Modern Babies

There was some excitement in the push chair.
Jason, nine months old, had cut his first tooth.
He picked up his mobile phone and tried to call
his little friend Sofie, exactly his age.

'Did you get her?' Mummy asked.

Jason shook his head. 'She was phoning the
tooth fairy.'

BRIAN ALDISS

Commissioned Story

Boy Meets Girl Except Without the Requisite Proof

She thought, he looked equal and tilted,
compact as a . . . sum. He thought she looked
exotic.

He said, I'd call you, but my illusions are vivid,
no less solid than wood. She sculpted each digit
in cigarette smoke.

Except it rained. When she'd gone, he had less
evidence than before.

DAVID OGUNMUYIWA
London SE17

Lovebirds

They had been careful. Very careful. She wore no perfume, didn't smoke in the house or apply lipstick until she had finished with a cup or glass. All went concealed. Until one silent, matrimonial evening, his pet (a Yellow-Crowned Amazon) mute for years and thought deaf, decided to talk . . .

STEPHEN BONE
Brighton

Love Letters

They met through the personal column, wordplay the mutual attraction. For years, they Scrabbled with a passion, exchanged crosswords (never angry ones) and shuffled magnetic letters into colourful protestations of love. Today, his pronouncement hangs invisibly in the air as he carelessly tosses all the right words into his suitcase.

TRACEY KENT
Horsham

The End of the Affair

'He said I'd sold my soul for sixpence,' she said, fingering through a sheaf of credit card statements.

'Bastard,' I said.

She paused to tug at her Armani skirt, smoothing it flat over well-toned thighs. 'Actually,' she said, 'what I've done is to sell my shares for six good fucks.'

ALISON CLAYBURN
London SE16

Any Way the Wind Blows

'Yes, John, a red heart-shaped balloon, with a message. It floated onto the terrace as your Mother and I had coffee.' June Vazakerly watched the colour rush to his face. 'It read – May our love always be light as air, signed Joy Wright and John Vazakerly and seven kisses.'

CHRIS COOPER
Huish Episcopi

Leopards

Walking down the street one day, the local miser, totally and hopelessly, fell madly in love with the lollipop lady.

'He'll change,' she told her friends, sceptical each and every one.

Still they attended the wedding and, afterwards, the reception.

The bill for the banquet arrived.

'They're your friends,' he muttered.

MICHAEL WHARTON
London W12

The Pyrrhic Victory

'Don't feed him; he has no reflux, since the accident,' said the nurse, unfastening the drip.

'We know,' said the plaintiff's sons.

When they got him home and gave him toast, he choked and died. His long-time mistress, the sole beneficiary under his will, inherited the million-dollar damages award.

CHRISTINE E. ADAMSON
Sydney, Australia

Supplies!

Wrapped inside a giant parcel, he posted himself
to his girlfriend, armed with chocolates, truffles,
caviar and champagne. He survived being
manhandled by the Post Office, savaged by
a dog . . . he even avoided suffocation.
Tragically, his sweetheart opened the package
with a twelve-inch samurai sword. Luckily,
it didn't ruin the supplies.

DAMON CRANE
Brighton

Kiss. Or, Leave Me Forever?

Once upon a time there was a clock. I gave it to you as a gift. It had no hands and no gubbins. Still it was beautiful.

'Why?' You asked.

'Our love's timeless.' I answered.

'And impractical.' You added.

You looked at your watch and said it was time to . . .

JOHN HEGLEY

Commissioned Story

United. Untied.

'Let's celebrate, darling,' said the anagram crossword compiler. 'It's our Silver Wedding.'

'Silver . . .' she mused, sipping champagne. '. . . key word . . .'

'Sliver!' she garbled, choking on a shard of glass.

'Olive!' he purred.

'Olive . . .?' she mused. 'I love . . .? O' evil . . .?'

The solution? A scarf made from voile. Tightened.

Her present, his future.

Peter C. Baruffati
Dundee

Home Is in the Head

He took string from his pocket.

She watched. He wove a house between his hands.

She closed her eyes. The house grew solid. Smoke curled from the chimney. A toddler played on the doorstep. With yards of ribbon he created a garden.

She looked at him, love in her eyes.

H. N. Chiswell
Weymouth

Listen to Mother?

'Never chase a man.' She remembered her mother's words.

Every evening he came, and they talked until closing. Then, as he left, 'I'm going away,' he said.

Consternation! Never see him again? Hesitation. She sped down the road.

Later that year: 'Best thing she ever did,' declared his admiring mother-in-law.

EDNA GRIFFIN
Fetcham

The Rock of Love

The day the phone call came through gave us great hope for the future. At last we can adopt a baby.

Where are all those doubters now? This musically talented and clever daughter loves us.

Wherever she goes and whatever she does in life, we will be there: her rocks.

M. BURROWS
Llandyrnog

Lovers Leap

He poses, resplendent in the shimmering light, dazzled by the glistening water. Skin shining, eyes aglow and throat murmuring his appreciation. Purposeful, waiting his moment.

His chance comes. She swims past. His muscles tense and flex, and he dives.

Leisurely the two amphibians seek their union under the lily pad.

SUSAN COOKE
Bolter End

Commended

Like Father, Like Son?

'Two questions, Dad. How do I get a girlfriend, and –

'– Treat her badly and *she'll* chase *you*. Stand her up. Undermine her confidence. Criticise her, and I guarantee she'll fall for you. Does that answer your question?'

'It answers both questions.'

'What was the second?'

'Why is Mum leaving you?'

GRAHAM DIX
King's Norton

The Secret Wardrobe

Alone at last . . . What a mess, smudged mascara, crooked eye liner and lipstick too red! Mind you, bra and dress look good and the shoes match. My legs need waxing and toe nails need painting. But no time now.

I'd better get this lot off before my wife comes home!!

R. G. BURROWS
Macclesfield

Commended